$$\frac{1}{4}$$

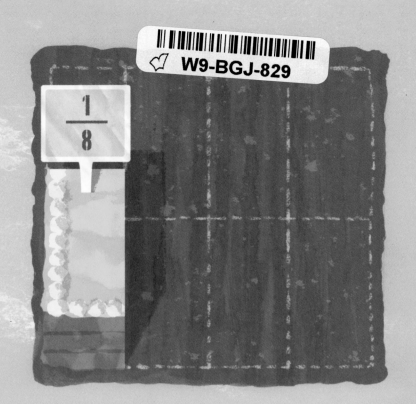

$$\frac{1}{8}$$

$$\frac{1}{64}$$

$$\frac{1}{128}$$

THE
LION'S
SHARE

MATTHEW McELLIGOTT

WALKER & COMPANY
NEW YORK

For Christy and Anthony

First published in the United States of America in 2009 by Walker Publishing Company, Inc.
Visit Walker & Company's Web site at www.walkeryoungreaders.com

For information about permission to reproduce selections from this book, write to
Permissions, Walker & Company, 175 Fifth Avenue, New York, New York 10010

Library of Congress Cataloging-in-Publication Data
McElligott, Matthew.
The lion's share / Matthew McElligott.
p.   cm.
Summary: Ant is honored to receive an invitation to lion's annual dinner party, but is shocked when the other guests
behave rudely and then accuse her of thinking only of herself.
ISBN-13: 978-0-8027-9768-1 ✦ ISBN-10: 0-8027-9768-7 (hardcover)
ISBN-13: 978-0-8027-9769-8 ✦ ISBN-10: 0-8027-9769-5 (reinforced)
[1. Behavior—Fiction. 2. Etiquette—Fiction. 3. Dinners and dining—Fiction. 4. Ants—Fiction. 5. Lions—Fiction.
6. Jungle animals—Fiction.] I. Title.
PZ7.M478448Lio 2009   [E]—dc22   2008013358

Book design by Nicole Gastonguay
Typeset in Sunshine
Art created with watercolor, ink, and digital techniques

Printed in China by C&C Offset Printing Co Ltd., Shenzhen, Guangdong
(hardcover) 10 9 8 7 6 5 4 3
(reinforced) 10 9 8 7 6 5 4 3

All papers used by Walker & Company are natural, recyclable products made from wood grown in well-managed forests.
The manufacturing processes conform to the environmental regulations of the country of origin.

Every year, at the start of spring, the lion
invited a small group of animals to join him for
a special dinner.

The ant had never dined with the king before. She was very nervous and wanted to make a good impression.

When the day came, she arrived exactly on time—not a minute too soon or too late.

When dinner was served, the ant was shocked at how the others behaved. The elephant talked about himself constantly. The hippo never wiped her mouth. The gorilla threw his food, and the warthog tried to eat the flowers.

"What strange manners," thought the ant. She looked to the lion, who said nothing.

After dinner, the table was cleared and a large cake was brought out for dessert. The lion passed it to the elephant.

"Please help yourself," he said.

The elephant looked at the cake. "I could eat this in one bite," he thought, "but that might seem greedy."

With a grand gesture, he **cut the cake in half** and passed the rest to the hippo.

"What a pig," thought the hippo. "But if he's taking half, I'm taking

half of what's left."

She made a slice

down the middle . . .

. . . and handed the remaining

one quarter

of the cake to the gorilla.

This continued around the table . . .

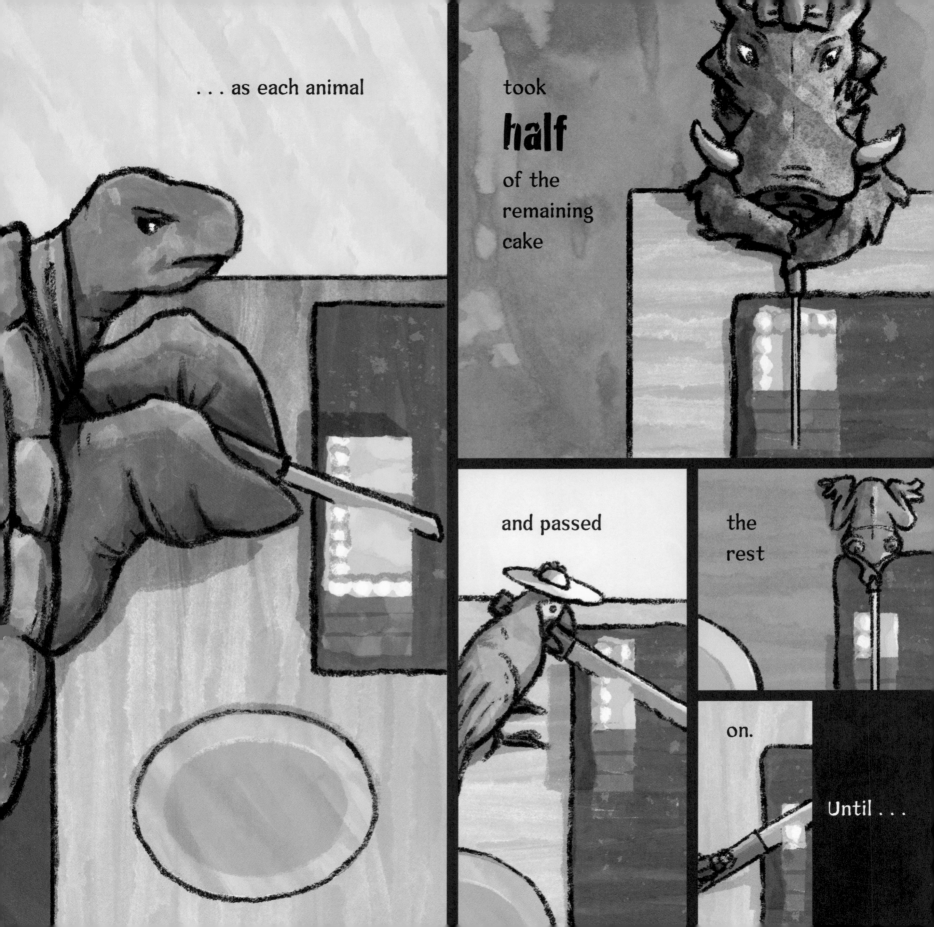

. . . it finally reached the ant. As she struggled to cut the

tiny slice in two,

it crumbled to pieces on her plate. All the animals turned to her.

"Typical ant," said the elephant. "She thinks only of herself. When the cake came to me, I shared it."

"I know," said the hippo. "We all did."

"Doesn't she know the king hasn't eaten yet?" scoffed the tortoise.

The warthog, who was sitting in her cake, simply shook her head in disgust.

The ant was mortified. Surely, she would never be invited back.

"My king," said the ant, "please forgive me. I am ashamed to say there is nothing left to share. But if you will allow, it would be my honor to bake a special strawberry sponge cake just for you tomorrow. It is my grandmother's recipe, and I think you will enjoy it."

The king smiled. "Thank you," he said. "You are very generous."

"Who does she think she is?" thought the beetle. He scampered over to the lion's plate.

"My king, to show *my* thanks, I would like to bake you

two

cakes tomorrow, double-chocolate fudge."

"Hey, King," said the frog. "I'm going to bake you

four

raspberry layer cakes tomorrow. That's *twice* as many!"

"I can top that," announced the macaw. "I shall bake the king twice as many carrot cakes:

eight!

And he shall have them tomorrow."

"Then I'll bake twice as many mud cakes," snorted the warthog. "How many is that, exactly?"

"Sixteen,"

said the tortoise.

"Really?" said the warthog. "That sounds like a lot."

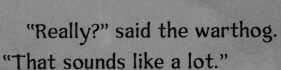

"Maybe for you," said the tortoise, "but I will happily bake twice that.

Thirty-two

apple-walnut cakes will be ready by tomorrow afternoon!"

The gorilla looked at the tortoise. He didn't like the tortoise. And although the gorilla had never baked anything ever before, he somehow found himself offering twice as many banana crumb cakes.

"Sixty-four?"

asked the king. "Are you sure?" The gorilla nodded, but he didn't look sure.

All eyes turned to the hippo.

"Naturally," she stammered, "it will be my honor to bake twice as many spice cakes. Let me see . . ."

She took out a piece of paper and began to scribble some numbers. Her hoof was shaking as she put down the pencil.

"This can't be right," she said finally.

The gorilla grabbed the piece of paper.

"One hundred and twenty-eight!"

he announced with a grin.

The elephant was crestfallen, but he had to top the hippo. Elephants were twice as good as hippos.

With a deep breath, he announced, "And I, the great elephant, shall bake twice as many as the hippo. Two hundred and forty-six peanut-butter pound cakes!"

"Two hundred and fifty-six,"

corrected the tortoise.

"Oh, for goodness' sake," cursed the elephant.

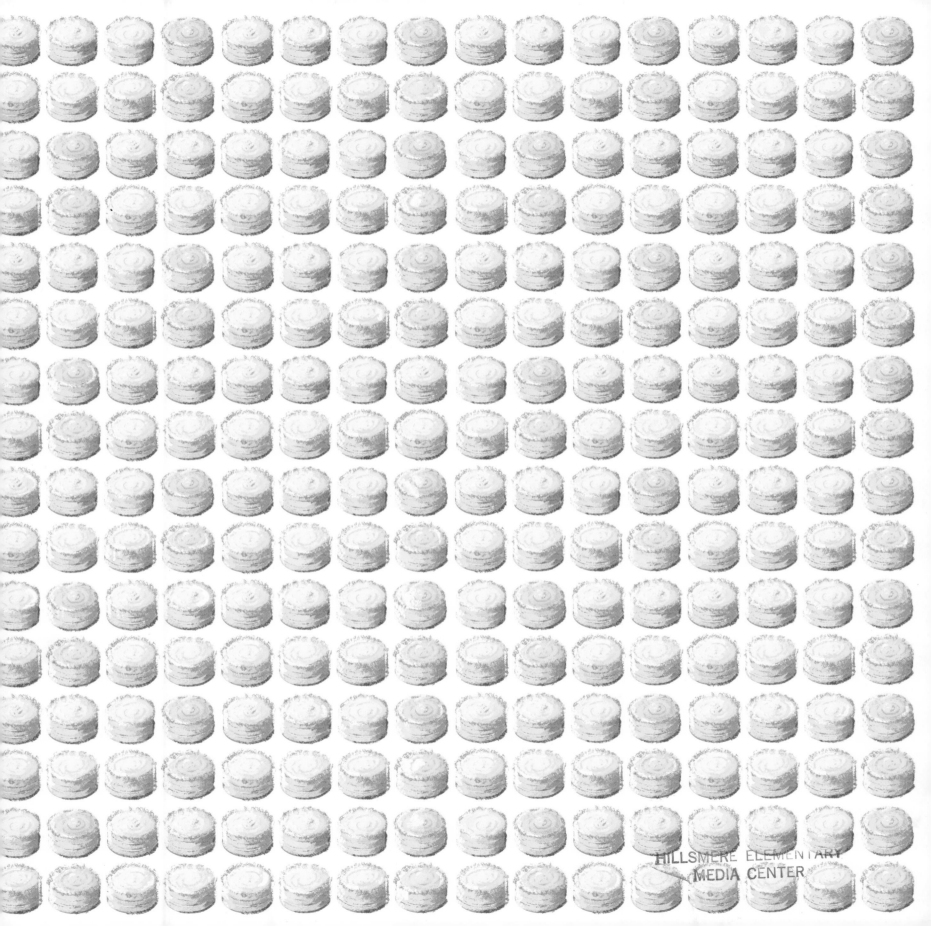

That night, the ant baked her cake
for the king. She took her time and
measured everything carefully. She
spread the frosting as smoothly as
she could, then decorated the top
with sprinkles. It was a very fine cake.

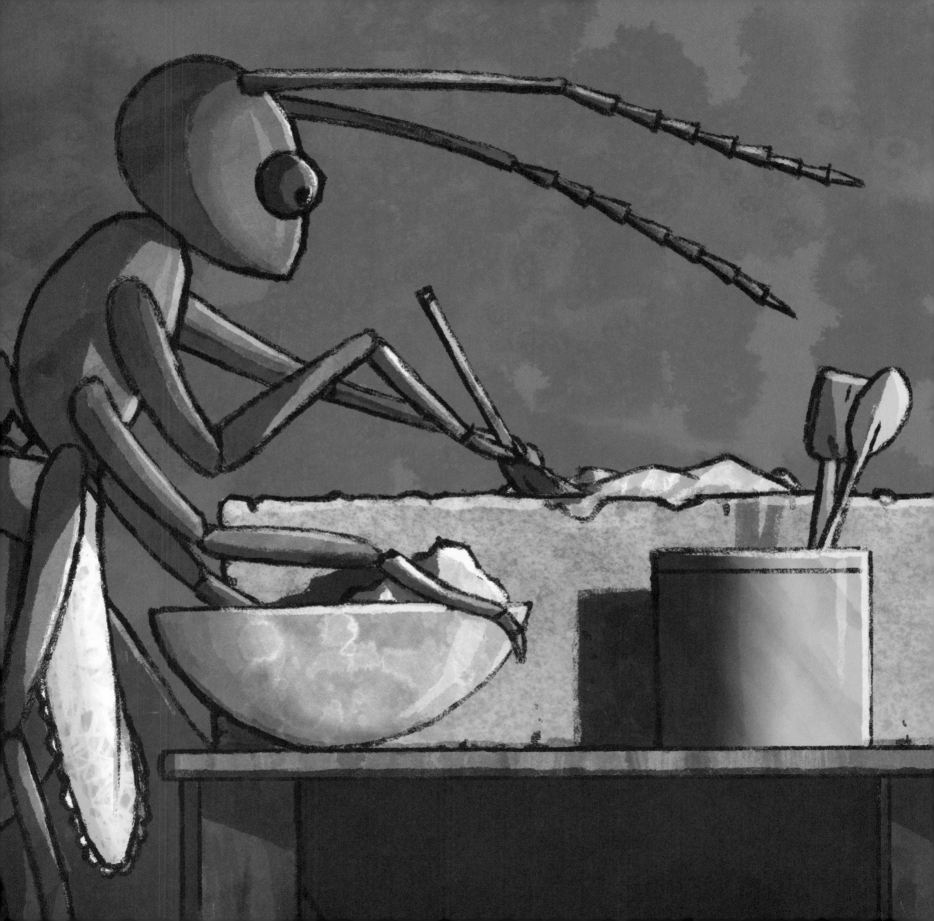

The next morning, she delivered it to the king.

"Such a fine cake," said the lion. "Won't you share it with me?"

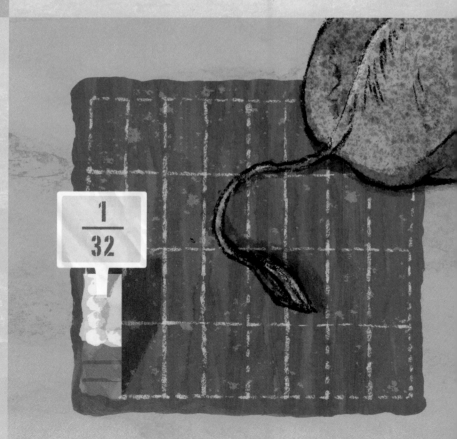